W9-BYL-035

DISCARD

Story by

Jill Paton Walsh

LOST AND FOUND

Illustrations by

Mary Rayner

ANDRE DEUTSCH

First published 1984 by
André Deutsch Limited
105–106 Great Russell Street London WC1B 3LJ
Third impression 1987

ISBN 0 233 97672 8
Printed in Hong Kong.

Mother said, "Come here, Little Ag. I have a job for you. Here is an arrowhead. Your father made it; your grandfather needs it. I would take it myself, but I am too busy with the new baby. Will you take it for me?"

"Yes," said Little Ag.

"Are you sure you know the way?" asked Mother.

"The way to Grandpa's hut?" said Little Ag. "Of course I know it!"

"Then here is the arrowhead. Hold it tight; be sure not to drop it. And be there and back as quickly as you can."

Little Ag took the arrowhead tight in his
right hand. He ran down the hill, below
the Great King's tomb, and through the
scrubby wood to the river shallows. He
splashed, plashed through the chilly river,
and came to the causeway over the marsh on
the other side. Little Ag liked plashing
through the river shallows, so he did it again,
two or three times. And the third time he
dropped the arrowhead, right into the
tumbling water.

Little Ag looked, and looked, and
looked for it, all among the wet and shiny
stones, but he could not find it.

But while he was looking he found
a round white stone, with a hole
in it, all the way through. Little
Ag put his finger through the hole,
and waggled it. Then he gave up
looking for the arrowhead, and went
towards Grandpa's hut, feeling very
worried all the way.

He went across the causeway over the marshy ground and up
the hill on the far side of the river, past the bank that
kept the cattle in, and past the wooden henge on the high
hilltop, and across the meeting-ground, to the row of huts,
one, two, three, four and five, where Grandpa lived.

"Have you brought my arrowhead, Little Ag?" asked Grandpa.

"I brought it, but I lost it on the way," said Little Ag, hanging his head.

"That is bad news, Little Ag," said Grandpa. "I can make an arrowhead for myself, if I have to, but losing one is bad, bad luck."

"While I was looking for it, I found this," said Little Ag, and he showed Grandpa the stone with the hole in it.

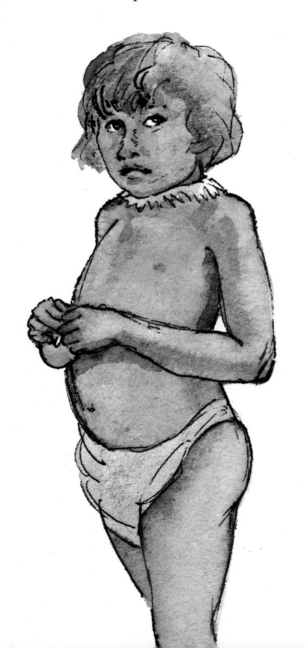

"Ha!" said Grandpa. "That's better! The ring stone is
very *good* luck, Little Ag, very strong magic."

"I shall give it to you, Grandpa, and it will
keep away the bad luck from losing your arrowhead," said
Little Ag.

"Then I shall hang it up over the door, and I shall
have nothing to worry about, Grandson," said Grandpa. "I
have a hare roasting over the fire, and ready to eat. Are
you hungry?"

"I am very hungry," said Little Ag. "Luck losing
and luck finding is hard work, Grandpa!"

"Eat up then," said Grandpa, "and off with you back
again, before your mother begins to worry."

Father said, "Come here, Sweet Alysoun, I have a job
for you. Here is a jug of fine fresh cream. Your mother
made it from our own cow's milk, and your grandmother
needs it. I would take it myself, but I am too busy making a
cradle for the new baby. Will you take it for me?"

"Yes," said Alysoun.

"Are you sure you know the way?" asked Father.

"The way to Gramma's cot?" said Alysoun. "Of course
I know it!"

"Then here is the jug of cream. Hold tight; be sure
not to spill it. And be there and back as quickly as you
can."

Sweet Alysoun took the jug tightly in both her hands. She walked down the hill, below Old Henga's Tump, and into the cool greenwood. Alysoun liked the wood, she liked to run round the trees, in and out. She had to be sure not to spill the jug of cream, so she put it carefully down in a very safe sort of place at the foot of a tree, and then she ran round and round and in and out. When she had finished running, she could not find the jug! Which tree had she put it by? There were so many, and all so much alike!

Alysoun looked, and looked, and *looked* for it, all among
the greenwood trees, and she could not find it.

Alysoun walked out of the greenwood, and over the
ford, by the stepping stones, to the far bank of the river,
and there on a little pebble beach she sat down and cried.
While she was crying she saw a funny shaped stone, lying
among the others on the river beach. It looked exactly
like a leaf. She picked it up. It was sharp at both
ends and all down both sides. Alysoun stopped crying,
and went on her way. She went along the marsh bank, and
up the hill, past Castle Farm field, full of cows, and
past the church on its high hilltop, and across the market
acre to the row of cottar's homes, one, two, three, four,
five, where her Gramma lived.

"Have you brought my jug of cream, Sweet Alysoun?" her Gramma asked.

"I was bringing it, and I put it down somewhere along the way, and I lost it," said Alysoun, hanging her head.

"Saints-a-mercy, Alysoun!" said Gramma. "I can drink water instead of cream if I must, but what a thing to do to so poor a dame as I am!"

"I have cried already, Gramma," Alysoun said. "And while I was crying, all sitting at the river side, I found this little pointed thing among the other stones."

"What's that?" cried Gramma. "Elfshot? You have found elfshot, child — a fairy arrowhead, that brings good luck and luck again to anyone who owns it."

"Then I shall give it to you, Gramma, instead of the jug of cream," said Alysoun.

"Thank you, Grand-daughter," said Gramma. "Now sit down to the fireside, and eat up an oaten cake and some honey before you go home again. I expect you are hungry enough for that."

"Oh yes, I am," said Alysoun.

"Eat up then, child. And be back with you, before your father thinks to worry."

"Come here to me, Peterkin," Mother said. "I have an errand for you. Here is sixpence that I owe to your grandfather. He needs it today, to go to market with it; but I am too busy to take it, what with the baby to see after. Can you take it for me?"

"Yes," said Peterkin.

"Are you sure you know the way?" asked Mother.

"The way to Grandfather's house?" said Peterkin. "Of course I know it."

"Then here is the sixpence. Keep it safe. Be sure not to lose it. And be there and back as quickly as you can."

Peterkin took the sixpence tight in his right hand. He ran down the hill, below Henny's Hump, and through the wood to the bridge across the river.

Then he ran up the hill, past Castle Farm cottages,
all up Marsh Lane nearly to the church on its high hilltop,
and then he opened his clenched fist, and found
he had lost the sixpence!

Peterkin went back every step of the way he had
come, looking and looking.

All the way back, almost to his own door he went, head down, looking and looking for a little speck of silver shine upon the path. And then back again towards Grandfather's house, and he looked specially hard on the track through the wood, where the sun might not reach to make the sixpence shine.

And while he was looking for the sixpence, all by the edge of the path, he saw a squirrel digging, and he went very close in case the squirrel had covered the sixpence over, and he saw a jug handle in the squirrel's hole. So he pulled at it, and up came a funny green and yellow jug, not even cracked! Peterkin took the jug, and went on looking for the sixpence, all the way across the bridge, and up the lane till he got nearly to the church on its high hilltop.

Then he stopped looking, but went on his way across the thronged and busy market in the square, to the terrace row, one, two, three, four and five, where Grandfather lived.

"Have you brought me me sixpence, young Peterkin?" asked Grandfather.

"I can't think how, and I can't think when, Grandfather," said Peterkin, hanging his head. "But I lost it upon the way, and I *cannot* find it."

"But what is that in your hand, Grandson?" asked Grandfather.

"This is what I found while I was looking for the sixpence, Grandfather," said Peterkin. "It is for you, if you want it."

"Well, what a piece of luck!" said Grandfather. "For it was to buy me a jug in the market that I needed the sixpence today, Peterkin, because I have broken the jug that fetches home ale from the inn. And this is a curious and ancient jug, and I like it better by far than a new one, so there is the harm put right. Wash it out under the pump, Peterkin, and draw up a stool to the table, and get some cold beef in your belly, before you run home again."

"I am very hungry," said Peterkin.

"A thick slice for you, then, boy," Grandfather said.

Mother said, "Jenny, come here, I have a job for you. Today is your nan's birthday, and I have bought her a new pair of scissors. But I haven't had time to wrap them, and I haven't the time to take them to her, what with nappies to wash, and the baby to take to the clinic. Can you take them for me, now, just as they are, and be quick about it?"

"Yes," said Jenny.

"Do you know the way?" Mother asked.

"The way to Nan's house?" said Jenny. "Of course I know it!"

"Then here are the scissors. Hold them loosely, points down, in case you should fall and hurt yourself.

And don't you dawdle and daydream. I want you back here
by twelve."

Jenny took the pair of scissors, loosely, points down,
in her right hand, and ran off down the hill. She went
through the car park for visitors to the stone age barrow,
and down the woodland path in the Town Park to the bridge.

She went across the footbridge,
below the bypass flyover . . .

along Bridge Street and under the railway arch, and up the hill, and past the Church into the market square.

Just at the side of the square some men were digging up the cobble-stones. Jenny stopped to watch, and to listen to the horrible noise their machine digger was making. She saw something round and black on the pile of earth by the hole. She put the scissors down for a moment, and picked up the round black thing. It was money — a coin — but not one Jenny knew. She put it deep in her pocket and then she couldn't find the scissors! They had *gone*! She looked, and looked, and *looked* all round where she had been standing, but she couldn't see them. She tried to ask the men, but they couldn't hear her.

The church clock struck a quarter past eleven.

Jenny began to cry. She cried all the way across the
market square to the council houses, one, two, three,
four, five, where her nan lived.

"What a way to say good morning, child" said Jenny's
Nan. "Whatever is the matter?"

"I lost your birthday present, Nan," said Jenny.
"I only put it down for a moment, to pick up this, and
then I couldn't find it."

"But just look what you did find, Jenny," said Nan.
"This is a very old sixpence indeed, child, real silver
money with some King George on the back. I shall rub
it up bright and shiny, and keep it for a pudding charm
and Christmas."

"Do you like it better than a new pair of scissors?"
said Jenny, drying her eyes.

"Much better, my duck, I have three pairs of
scissors already. And I've got Danish and doughnuts
for elevenses. I shall ring up your mother at once, and
tell her you're stopping for a while. I shall say that
scissors always come in handy, which is perfectly true.
And the sixpence shall be our secret. Is that better?"

"Nan, you're *great*!" said Jenny.

"All things in their time, child," said Nan.